Commit to the Lord whatever you do,

and your plans will succeed.

—Proverbs 16:3

ZONDERKIDZ

The Berenstain Bears Do Their Best
Previously published by Reader's Digest Kids in 1992 as *The Berenstain Bears and the Big Red Kite*
Copyright © 1992, 2010 by Berenstains, Inc.
Illustrations © 1992, 2010 by Berenstains, Inc.

Requests for information should be addressed to:

Zonderkidz, Grand Rapids, Michigan 49530

Library of Congress Cataloging-in-Publication Data

Berenstain, Stan, 1923–2005
    The Berenstain Bears do their best / created by Stan and Jan Berenstain ; with
Mike Berenstain.
        p.   cm.
    Summary: Papa and the Bear cubs enter a kite flying contest with a homemade kite and, with
God's help, they do their best and win despite taunting from some of the other contestants.
    ISBN 978-0-310-71937-3 (hardcover)
    [1. Stories in rhyme. 2. Kites—Fiction 3. Perseverance (Ethics)—Fiction. 4. Christian life—Fiction.
5. Bears—Fiction.] I. Berenstain, Jan, 1923- II. Berenstain, Michael. III. Title.
    PZ8.3.B4493Bhc 2010
    [E]—dc22   2009037061

Editor: Mary Hassinger
Art direction: Cindy Davis

Printed in USA

11 12 13 14 15 16 /WPW/ 29 28 27 26 25 24 23 22 21 20 19 18 17 16 15 14 13 12 11 10 9 8 7 6 5 4

The Berenstain Bears

Do Their Best

by Stan and Jan Berenstain
with Mike Berenstain

ZONDERVAN.com/
AUTHORTRACKER
follow your favorite authors

ZONDERkidz

Living
Lights™

Look, Sister Bear!
Hooray! Hooray!
The big kite contest
is today!

BIG
KITE
CONTEST
TODAY!

Yes, Brother Bear.
I see. That's right.
But we can't go.
We have no kite!

No kite? No kite?
Now, do not worry.
I can make one
in a hurry!

A kite for me and Sister Bear?
A kite for both of us to share?
Let's thank the Lord from up above
for Papa showing us his love.

I'll make a kite.
Just wait and see,
with the special talents
God gave me!

First some sticks—
just two will do.
Some paper, string,
and a little glue.

We tie.

We cut.

Now, we glue.
See? I made a kite
for you!

A big red kite!
It's a beauty!
Big Red Kite,
do your duty!

It sure is red.
No doubt about it.
But will it fly?
I really doubt it.

For, you see,
without a tail,
that big red kite
is sure to fail.

This old bed sheet
will make a tail.

This tail will help
Big Red to sail.

Kite contest,
we're on our way!
Our big red kite
will win the day!

Kites! Kites!
Up ahead!

Are any as special
as our Big Red?

Kites of every
shape and size
sail and dance
across the skies—

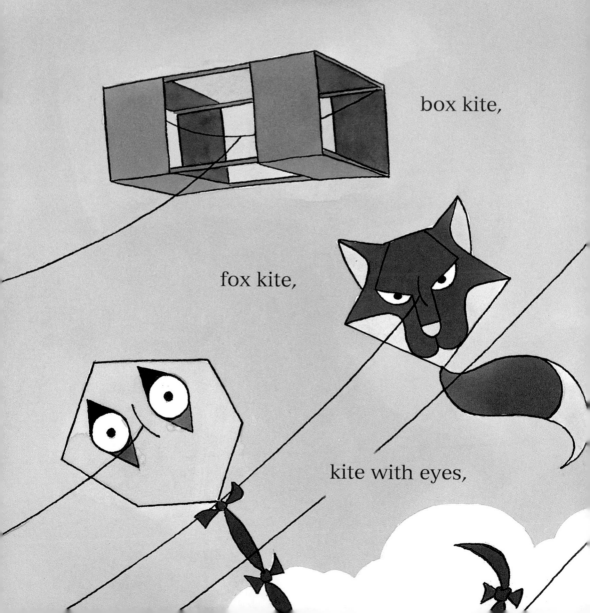

box kite,

fox kite,

kite with eyes,

kites that look like butterflies,

a dragon with
a long green tail,

a kite that says:
SAVE THE WHALE.

The judge looks
down his nose at Red.
"It looks homemade,"
the kite judge said.

Oh? Oh?

Is that so?

It's time to fly?

Here we go!

Run, Papa! Run!
Have faith! Be tough!
But are hope and prayer
going to be enough?

We won't give up!
We'll keep on trying.
Red will soon
be up and flying!

Look, Papa! Look!
The wind grows strong!

In wind like this,
those fancy kites
will not last long!

Look! Red flies high,
and higher still!

I know we'll win!
I know we will!

That wind is strong.
That wind is rough.
Those other kites
weren't strong enough!

But we believed
in Papa's skill.
And our faith in God's help
is stronger still.

Big Red has won
fair and square.
Congratulations,
Papa Bear!

You believed,
you did your best
and that took Red
higher than the rest!

We won! We won,
Mama Bear!

Our big red kite
won fair and square!

You passed a very
important test:
You didn't quit!
You did your best.
Papa, Brother, and Sister,
you are very blessed!

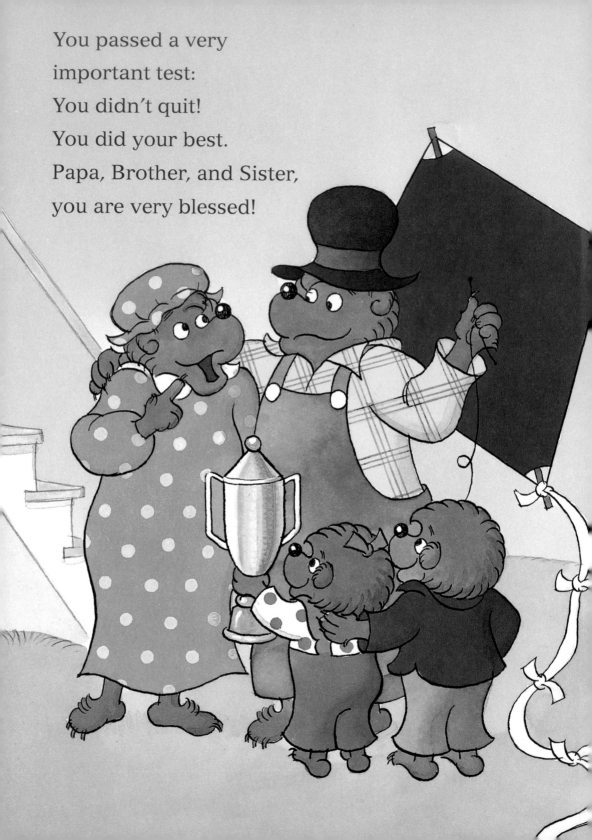